THE HAUNTING
OF
APARTMENT 612

A PARANORMAL MYSTERY

E.M. PARKER

SECOND
SIGHT
PUBLISHING

1

THE NEW TENANT

THE THING IN THE PIT OF MY STOMACH MADE ITSELF known the instant I woke up this morning. I called it a *thing* because I wasn't sure what else to label it. *Butterflies*, *fear*, and *outright dread* were the words that immediately came to mind, but those were obvious choices and did no justice to the feeling. This was something else entirely; something dark, heavy, and primordial. Like the murky residue of a long nightmare that ended with a brutal, mind-numbing swiftness.

Or maybe the nightmare was just beginning.

Whatever the *thing* was, there was nothing

I could point to that accounted for its existence.

As far as I remembered, my six hours of sleep were uneventful, with none of the bad dreams or other nighttime disturbances that had recently become such a common part of my life here.

I'd been up late cramming for an anatomy midterm that I was woefully underprepared for, and with the exam now only a few hours away, I couldn't outline the functions of the endocrine system any easier than I could map the stars of the solar system.

For a moment, I thought that this had been the source of the *thing*. But under preparing for exams was nothing new—a sad fact that I'd resolved to correct before my graduation this spring—and I'd always been able to pull off a passing grade, even if it was by the thinnest of margins. My chronic procrastination aside, I knew that I'd find a way to pass this one too.

That left no viable explanation for why it felt like the entire world was about to come crashing down on top of my head.

Then I heard the knock on the door.

I'd just begun a yoga session that I hoped would relieve my mounting anxiety. It took a full minute to ease into the King Pigeon pose that required me to bend backward until the edge of my brow touched the backs of my toes. The position was advanced, taking nearly two years to master. And now that I had, it was the go-to move whenever I needed to drown out the noise in my head. Right now, there was a lot of noise to drown out.

I barely had time to blink before the first series of knocks shattered my concentration.

Choosing to ignore the intrusion, I quickly regrouped, closed my eyes, and took in a deep breath, curving my spine another couple of inches until the tip of my nose settled into the mid-soles of my feet.

With my throat tightening and my brain filling with blood, I felt a blissful light-headedness that instantly dulled my heightened senses.

Within seconds, I was on another plane of time and space altogether. Far away from the fear of failed mid-terms. Far away from the barista job that I despised. Far away from the once inviting apartment building that was now cold, foreign, and lifeless. Far away from the *thing* in the pit of my stomach that told me to run away from it all.

Another series of knocks rattled the door before I could complete my mental escape. This series was much harder than the first, a clear indication that the intruder had no designs on being ignored a second time.

I slowly uncoiled my long, athletic frame, sighing with a force that I hoped was loud enough to convey my irritation.

"Who is it?" I said as I sprang to my feet.

"Phillip Barlow."

I cursed under my breath before taking a step to the door. My legs were wobbly, and I had to pause to allow my equilibrium to return. I wasn't sure if this was because I'd stood too fast or because my landlord, a man who rarely acknowledged anyone unless their rent was late or their television was too loud, had decided to pay an unscheduled visit. I was leaning toward the latter.

The thought caused the *thing* in my stomach to expand until it swelled inside my chest.

Barlow was smiling when I opened the door. He looked nervous.

Why would he be nervous?

The *thing* suddenly spread from my chest into the base of my throat.

"Morning, Norah."

"Mr. Barlow."

"I'd like to think that we've moved beyond formalities. Phillip will do." He gave me a once over, his eyes moving from my coral-colored toenails to my neon green yoga pants to the beads of sweat on my freckled face before adding, "I hope I didn't catch you at a bad time."

"Not at all," I lied, blowing a tangle of auburn hair from my forehead.

"That's good. I do apologize for stopping by unannounced. It's been a crazy morning and I'm afraid I didn't have time to phone ahead. Do you have a few minutes to talk?"

I fought to downplay my apprehension as I stepped into the hallway and closed the door to a crack. "Sure. What can I help you with?"

"May I come in?"

I opened the door and begrudgingly allowed space for him to walk through. "Of course."

He smiled politely as he moved past me and into the apartment.

Phillip Barlow was a tall, stout man, but his rounded shoulders and loose posture made him appear much shorter. His dark curly hair was long and unkempt on the sides and thinning to a few pitiful strands up top. It lay in stark contrast to a patchy gray beard that contained a few traces of the light brown that had most likely been his hair color before the dye job. The pale skin around his eyes folded when he smiled. It was a trait shared by my father. He reminded me a lot of my father, right down to the anxiety that his mere presence could inspire.

Barlow groaned as he helped himself to a seat on my futon. "Cozy space."

"It's not much, but it's home."

Aside from the futon that doubled as my bed, there was a loveseat, a coffee table that acted as my bookshelf, a dinette set that regularly hosted frozen dinners for one, and a small computer desk where I seemed to whittle away most of my time. There were a few family pictures scattered about, a picture of my ex-boyfriend that I hadn't gotten around to removing, and a Gray's Anatomy muscle diagram pinned to the main wall.

The space was far from impressive, but it served its purpose. I could have done without the sudden drafts of cold air, the strange noises that kept me awake at night, and the recent attention that that little girl's murder brought to the building. But beyond that, I couldn't complain. It was a place to live, and if the sports medicine job market was as robust as my professors promised, my stay here would only be temporary.

God willing.

"Well, it looks great," Barlow reiterated. "I do believe this is the first time I've been here since you officially moved in."

"I do believe you're right," I answered with a forced smile as I sat on the love seat adjacent to him.

"As a matter of fact, I don't think I've seen you since..." Barlow cut himself off, either unwilling or unable to finish the sentence. "How have you been?"

I drew in a sharp breath and held it.

Five months ago, the elderly tenant next door to me in Apartment 612 was found hanging from the doorway of his living room. I was the first person interviewed by the police.

They questioned me for half an hour, probing the depths of our relationship (there wasn't one), asking if I'd heard anything strange or seen anything out of the ordinary earlier that evening (I hadn't), and searching for any possible motive that would explain his death (like I had the first clue why he died).

Despite the ongoing police investigation and the horrifying events that followed, I'd never once seen Barlow. He didn't stop by to check up on me, offered no reassurances that the building was safe, despite my growing concern that it wasn't, and made no promises that things would eventually return to normal. I probably should have felt slighted by his indifference, but I didn't. I simply responded with an indifferent attitude of my own.

But now, as he made himself comfortable in my living room, unannounced, uninvited, and suddenly concerned, I felt a bitterness welling up inside of me that I struggled to suppress.

"I've been fine."

"That's good to hear. And is the apartment in good order? Any leaks that need fixing or holes that need patching?"

"I have hot water and the lights work. That's good enough."

Barlow gave a light chuckle before his eyes landed on the pile of textbooks atop my coffee table. "And how is school coming along?" He craned his neck to read the nearest title. "*Textbook of Sports Medicine: Basic Science and Clinical Aspects of Sports Injury and Physical Activity*. Wow. Sounds like a brain full."

"It is."

"Where are you going to school?"

"Metro State. I graduate this spring."

"Such an exciting time. What's your major?"

"Exercise science with a minor in sports medicine. I'd like to be a trainer, maybe catch on with a college or pro team at some point."

"That's fantastic. Best of luck."

Barlow was overselling his enthusiasm. He couldn't have cared less about me or my major. He was stalling, and I couldn't let it go on a second longer.

"I appreciate that, Mr. Barlow. Can I ask what brings you by?"

His expression flattened. "Right. I'm sure you have plenty to do, and I don't want to take up more of your time than I need to, so I'll get straight to it."

Instead of getting straight to it, Barlow sat back on the futon and crossed his legs. He cupped his raised foot to stop it from shaking. "I notice you don't have a television, so I'm not sure how much news you've seen lately."

"I avoid the news if I can help it. Too much negativity."

"I know what you mean. I probably watch more than I should. If something happens in the world, I feel like I'm better off being in the loop. Nine times out of ten, I'm wrong. Anyway, it's good that you've been steering clear of it, especially now. Our building has been getting its share of press lately, and unfortunately, none of it's been good."

His words sent a chill up my spine. "I don't need a television to know that. It's all that anyone around here can talk about."

"And that's the problem. People aren't just talking. They're spreading rumors that simply aren't true. I understand that residents are frightened and upset by what happened here. Hell, it's caused me more sleepless nights than I care to count. But to take such a tragedy as an opportunity to propagate wild conspiracy theories about the history of this building is flat out irresponsible. And now the media is starting to buy into the nonsense."

I was well-aware of the conspiracy theories that Barlow was referring to. By now, most everyone else in the building was too.

"Do you know that I was given an article just the other day that lists Corona Heights as the fifth most haunted location in the entire state?" he continued.

There was an awkward silence as if he were waiting for me to respond, so I did, sarcasm framing my words. "Wow, that's something."

"Most ridiculous thing ever if you ask me. But that story wasn't made up on a whim. Someone here is feeding that garbage to the public, and it's starting to have real life consequences. Tenants have been moving out in droves. In less than three years, we've gone from having a long waiting list to having one of the highest vacancy rates in the city. That wouldn't be an issue if people were clamoring to move in, but they aren't. I'm afraid that if the bleeding doesn't stop, the building will be sold and the good tenants like yourself will be out of a place to live. Which means I'll be out of a job."

That got my attention. The only reason I hadn't joined the droves who moved out was because of the rent. It was far and away the cheapest in the city, given the building's downtown location and proximity to campus. I would have been hard-pressed to find a deal like it anywhere else and wasn't the least bit prepared to try, despite my apartment's not-so-desirable features. "Could that really happen?"

"Absolutely. The owners are already losing money, and the more this haunted house garbage takes hold, the more of a liability this place becomes. Corona Heights has too much positive history to end up as some derelict tourist attraction. The owners are counting on me to ensure that doesn't happen."

"What are you going to do?"

"Rehab the building's image, for starters. We're planning some physical updates, both to the exterior and common interior areas, as well as the apartments themselves. Fresh energy should help brighten the perception among the existing tenants, which hopefully makes them less likely to scare off any prospective renters before they can give us a fair chance. The negative press is bad enough. We have no chance of staying afloat if we can't get our own residents to vouch for us."

"Do you really think that painting the walls a brighter color is going to be enough?"

Barlow looked surprised by my pointed question. "It's a good first step."

"What's your plan after that?"

He took in a deep breath and blew it out slowly as he edged forward on the futon. "That's why I'm here. I need your help."

"With what?"

"The new tenant."

"What new tenant?"

He took in another deep breath. This time, he didn't exhale. "The new tenant moving in next door to you."

"Someone is moving into 612?"

Barlow nodded. "Tomorrow morning."

The *thing* moved down my throat and chest and settled back into my stomach, the pain nearly causing me to double over. "After what happened in there, I figured you were keeping it vacant."

"Quite the contrary. I've been trying like crazy to rent it out. Unfortunately, it's been a tough sell. I've had four people come through in the past month alone looking for an apartment. As soon as I led them to 612, they promptly lost interest. Every single one of them."

"A man died in there, Mr. Barlow. Can you really blame them?"

"I don't blame them. I blame the whack-jobs who are spreading lies about *how* he died."

As far as I knew, Donald Tisdale committed suicide. There were plenty of reports to the contrary, fueled mostly by a former tenant named Fiona Graves, the resident psychic Iris Matheson, and the building's own sketchy history.

I'd done my best not to believe those reports, but I did know that something wasn't right inside that apartment. A cold energy seemed to radiate through the door every time I walked past it. Sometimes, late at night, that cold energy seeped through the walls and straight into my dreams.

I could never put my finger on what it was. I only knew that it was something very dark and very real, and it hadn't existed before Tisdale's death.

There was a reason why that apartment had been vacant all these months, and for the sake of everyone in the building, I'd hoped that it would remain vacant. Now that Barlow was telling me that it wouldn't, I knew exactly what he wanted me to do.

Even as he began speaking the words that confirmed it, I still held out hope that I was wrong.

"The tenant is new to Colorado, so I'm not sure if she's had a chance to read up on the place," Barlow said. "But if someone hasn't already put a bug in her ear, it's only a matter of time before they do. If it ever does come up, I'm asking you not to feed into the rumors. I don't expect you to lie. Something terrible did happen inside that apartment, and I was obligated to disclose that. I could tell that she was shaken, but it ultimately didn't affect her decision to move in. She's open-minded, and I'd like to keep it that way."

"What are you expecting me to say if she asks about it? The ghost stuff, I mean."

"Have you ever had an experience that leads you to believe the building is haunted?"

I had to think about it a moment longer than I should have, and even then, I still wasn't completely confident. "Not that I'm aware of."

"Then that's what you tell her. You live next door to the supposed epicenter of Corona Heights's supernatural activity. Your skepticism will carry a lot of weight. It's vital to have that apartment occupied. But it's even more important that the new tenant stays. I need your help to make sure that happens."

"But what if she really does experience something in there?"

"Like what? A strange noise?"

I bristled at his response. "I hear things all the time."

"This building is well over a hundred years old. It creaks, it groans, the pipes rumble, and the insulation is terrible. The only real danger that anyone faces around here is catching a cold in the winter because it gets so drafty. Trust me, she doesn't have anything to worry about, and neither do you."

It would have been nice to hear those words five months ago, but for the sake of expediting Barlow's exit, I was willing to accept his reassurance. "I'll do my best to convey the message."

"That would make me, and the owners, very happy."

With that, Barlow stood up and made his way to the door. I followed close behind, eager to show him out.

"I know it may sound like a strange request," he said as he opened the door. "And on the surface, I suppose it is. But I can't tell you how much it will mean to have things return to normal around here. Having someone in there who can directly refute this supernatural craziness will go a long way in doing that. Thank you for helping."

Did I really have a choice? was what I thought. "No problem," was what I said.

Barlow nodded and started down the hallway.

I barely had time to close the door before there was another knock. I opened it to the sight of a smiling Barlow.

"Sorry to bug you again, but I forgot to mention something. The new tenant's name is Cassandra Scott. She's a young girl, about your age. Really nice. The two of you should get along wonderfully." He started down the hall again. "Like I said, we really appreciate this. If you need anything at all, please don't hesitate to ask."

The absence of air in my lungs only allowed for a tight smile.

When Barlow left for good, I closed the door then leaned against it for support, fearful that my already wobbly legs would give out completely.

Cassandra Scott.

The thing in the pit of my stomach finally had a name.

2

A FAMILIAR CHILL

MOST OF WHAT HAPPENED AFTER BARLOW'S departure was a blur. I remembered showering, getting dressed, biking the usual six miles to campus, and fumbling through my midterm, but the details of those events were difficult to recall.

The memories of my five hours at work were even less accessible. I knew that I stood behind the counter of the City Perk Café with my usual fake cheeriness, churning out one soy decaf latte after another. But I couldn't recollect a single interaction beyond that. All I could think about was Barlow's visit, his odd request, and the new tenant that I had essentially been tasked with babysitting.

In the best-case scenario, Cassandra Scott would end up being a hardcore skeptic who dismissed any suggestion of the paranormal the moment she heard it. But given the recent history of Corona Heights in general and Apartment 612 in particular, the odds of outright dismissal weren't good.

I may have been nothing more than a babysitter, but the weight of the responsibility suddenly felt heavy, and I resented Barlow for not asking someone else.

Once the last decaf latte had been blended and my painfully long shift was over, I made my way back home.

The building was quiet when I arrived. It usually was at this late hour. Still, I kept my head down as I entered the first-floor lobby.

I was somewhat famous around Corona Heights for being the unfortunate soul who lived next door to 612, and with word likely spreading that the apartment would finally be occupied, I anticipated that the probing from the gossip mongers would be intense.

Thankfully, I didn't see anyone as I climbed inside the waiting elevator.

A familiar chill set in as I made the short

walk to my apartment. It normally resulted in little more than a brief shudder that passed once 612 was out of sight. Tonight, the chill lingered, burrowing under my skin and into my veins where it traveled unfettered into every corner of my body.

The chill only intensified when I entered my apartment. The air outside was cool and crisp, typical of late October, but the inside was frigid.

I immediately checked the kitchen window. Seeing that it was closed, I walked over to what must have surely been a broken thermostat. It was set to its normal sixty-eight degrees. I turned it up a few notches, then held my hands over the radiator as if I were warming them over a crackling fire. It took several minutes, but the chill finally broke.

After a hot shower and a plate of cold pasta, I settled in at my desk. My next midterm was less than a week away, and I thought it wise to be proactive in my preparation this time.

I blew a mound of dust off my *Pathology of Athletic Injury* textbook and cracked it open. It creaked like an ancient crypt being unlocked for the first time in centuries (or, in this case, for the first time since the start of the semester).

I stared intently at the notations and bright yellow highlights made by previous students, but I couldn't process anything that I was seeing. My thoughts were still on Barlow, the chill outside of 612, and the girl who was now hours away from moving in.

I couldn't stop asking myself why Barlow was so determined to have that particular apartment occupied. There were plenty of vacancies in the building, including a unit down the hall that was the scene of a death ten times worse than Tisdale's. Yet, Barlow seemed fixated on 612.

The rumors had obviously gotten to him despite his attempts to downplay them. But I could sense that something else had shaken him up. What was it? And why was he so sure that bringing in a new renter was the only way to alleviate his fear?

As much as I wanted to kick myself for not asking the question, I knew that he wouldn't have offered a straight answer anyway. If I truly wanted to know, I would have to take my own trip down the Donald Tisdale rabbit hole, something I hadn't been willing to do before now.

Ignorance truly was bliss in this case, but thanks to Barlow, it was a luxury that I could no longer indulge in.

3
THINGS THAT GO BUMP

My DESCENT DOWN THE RABBIT HOLE BEGAN WITH an internet search of Corona Heights. I added in the word *haunted* for good measure.

While some of the results came from legitimate outlets like the *Denver Post*, most were from independent news sites and blogs that specialized in the supernatural.

The headlines ranged from the ordinary (POLICE REFUSE TO RULE OUT FOUL PLAY IN ELDERLY MAN'S HANGING DEATH) to the sensational (MEET THE FAMILY OF FOUR THAT HAUNTS DENVER'S SCARIEST APARTMENT BUILDING). One website—*Things That Go Bump*—seemed to devote its entire existence to stories about Corona Heights.

There were interviews with frightened residents who claimed to see everything from the spirits of children roaming the hallways to winged humanoid creatures that burrowed their way in through tunnels in the sub-basement.

And the stories only got more ridiculous from there.

According to one, Corona Heights was once occupied by a coven of witches that regularly kidnapped and sacrificed the building's residents. Another claimed that it was the secret headquarters of an international group of devil worshipers who used the site as an active portal that led straight to the gates of Hell.

I found similar accounts in most of the other websites I visited. It was the kind of crackpot conspiracy-theory garbage that no one aside from its authors could ever take seriously.

For all the other positive attributes that Barlow was lacking, he was a reasonable, level-headed man, so it was hard to imagine that he was taking any of it seriously either.

But what if he was?

Moving on from the wasteland of tabloid

garbage, I expanded my query to include the words *Donald Tisdale* and *Apartment 612*.

The top result was another *Post* article that summarized the basics of Tisdale's suicide and the police investigation that followed.

The article shed little light on Tisdale's life, offering only his occupation as the night janitor at a local high school. There was no mention of his alleged connection to the seven-year-old girl whose decayed remains were recently found buried inside the walls of Apartment 605, or his close friendship with the man who was currently in police custody for her murder.

Another story from a small publication called the *Denver Daily Mail* went into greater detail about the Tisdale investigation, specifically the incidents that occurred inside the apartment while police were there.

The article featured an interview with an anonymous source within the department who knew the detectives assigned to the case.

According to the source, there were strange occurrences inside 612 almost immediately after the detectives arrived.

They found fresh pools of blood that appeared spontaneously in the kitchen and bedroom, they heard knocking inside the walls and ceiling that seemed to follow them wherever they went, and they saw moving shadows in the corners and behind doors.

But the most unnerving discovery was the trap door inside the floor of the bedroom closet.

The evidence found inside of it was enough to link the building's former maintenance supervisor to the girl whose dismembered body was discovered less than a day later. The source insisted that the trap door hadn't been there during previous searches of the room and had simply *"appeared out of nowhere when it was ready to be seen."*

Similar incidents occurred throughout the investigation that left the detectives wary of the apartment. One of those detectives, Chloe Sullivan, had even been quoted as saying that she would never again answer a call to Corona Heights, even if it cost her a job.

There was a lot more, including a story about the detective's confrontation with the spirit of the murdered girl and the *"psychic on the sixth floor"* who managed to stop her. But I suddenly decided that I'd had enough.

Even though I was skeptical of what I'd

read, I'd also had enough encounters with the unexplainable to be set on edge by every noise I heard or chill that I felt. This research wasn't helping, and I knew it was best to abandon it, and all the questions raised by Barlow's visit.

It had been a long, strange day and I needed to sleep it off. I would wake up to-morrow and go right back to my normal rou-tine. If I ran into Cassandra Scott, I would politely introduce myself and be on my way. I would wish her the best, of course, but there would be no reason to get involved beyond that.

I may have no longer had the luxury of blissful ignorance, but Cassandra did. Hope-fully, she would find a way to keep it.

After a quick meditation to dampen the racket in my head, I drifted off into a peaceful, dreamless sleep.

I was startled awake a few hours later by the sound of heavy footsteps in the hallway outside my apartment.

The only two units on this wing of the floor were 612 and mine, which meant that traffic was usually light. Anytime I heard a noise outside the door, especially at night, it commanded my full attention.

I sat up in bed, my ears tuned to the foot-steps, hoping that they would continue down the hall until they faded altogether. But instead of moving away from the door, the foot-steps drew closer before abruptly stopping.

The sliver of hallway light filtering in through the bottom of the door was suddenly darkened by movement. Then I heard the jiggle of a door handle followed by the light groan of squeaking hinges.

Someone was entering 612. It was 1:17 a.m.

4

AFRAID OF THE DARK

ALARMED BUT CURIOUS, I EASED OUT OF BED AND slowly approached the door. The light underneath continued to be blocked by a roving shadow, but there was no corresponding sound. No footsteps, no soft padding across the carpet, no squeaking hinges.

Before I could make it halfway, the shadow stopped moving. The darkness spread as it hovered outside my door.

Not believing what I was seeing, I stopped, rubbed the last remnants of sleep out of my eyes, and refocused them. The shadow was still there, slowly suffocating the sliver of hallway light until there was none left.

Somewhere in the darkness outside, I heard a man. His voice was distant, its soft tone echoing with an almost otherworldly resonance.

"We're finally here, princess. Exciting, isn't it?"

I held my breath in anticipation of a response. When I didn't hear one, I edged closer to the door. The shadow moved with me, allowing a single speck of light to peek inside.

"Don't worry. Mommy's coming soon. Why don't we go in and spruce up the place?"

His voice was closer now.

"Giving daddy the silent treatment, huh? Well, that cute smile tells me you're just as happy to be here as I am. I really hope she'll be happy too."

I jumped at the sound of cooing.

"There's my sweet girl."

At that, the baby grew more animated, its slurred inflections attempting a verbal response that it wasn't yet capable of articulating.

"Not too loud, honey bunch. You don't want to wake her before she has the chance to see you."

He laughed the way a proud, loving, perfectly harmless father was supposed to.

Barlow never mentioned anything about Cassandra Scott having a husband or baby. It was possible that she could have withheld the information on her first visit. But there would be no way to hide their presence once she moved in. More to the point, why would she choose to move in this time of night with an infant in tow? No mother in her right mind would ever do such a thing.

Not yet ready to concede that I was now living next door to a crazy person, I had to conclude that the baby wasn't Cassandra's.

So, if there was no husband or child living in 612, who was standing outside my door?

My thoughts immediately drifted to the darkest place imaginable.

There were no infants on this floor that I knew of. The only children I had ever heard of were Hannah Shelby, the murdered girl who once lived in 607, and her twin sister Olivia. Olivia was taken away after her mother's death five months ago. Some people believe Hannah never left.

As much as the thought shook me, I still

didn't want to believe the rumors of active ghosts any more than Barlow did.

And yet, there was something about that voice...

"*Come on, honey. Let's get started.*"

Something about that baby's innocent, playful excitement...

"*I know. Me too.*"

That wasn't natural.

"*Your mommy is afraid of the dark now. Thankfully, I never was. You take after me, don't you? A daddy's girl through and through.*"

There was a long silence followed by the sound of aching hinges. The door to 612 was opening again. There was a quick shuffle of movement, then the door slammed shut, its resonance forcing me back on my heels.

After taking a moment to collect myself, I made my way back to the door and the shadow that still lingered outside of it. The darkness shifted as I reached for the doorknob. When I touched it, the darkness disappeared, allowing a thin beam of light to spill inside my apartment.

I inhaled in short, spastic bursts as I looked through the peephole.

The space outside was empty.

My hand hovered over the doorknob for more than a minute before I found the courage to open it.

The chill hit me immediately, more intensely than before. But the hallway was quiet. No voices, no shadows, no footsteps.

I glanced at the closed door of 612 and tuned my ear to the silence, eager to pick up on any sign that someone was inside. If Cassandra had chosen to move in, ungodly as the hour was, the sound of movement would have been impossible to miss. But there was nothing.

I took a cautious step into the hallway, then another, and then another, until I was standing in front of 612, something I hadn't dared to do since Donald Tisdale's death.

The silence behind its walls was almost as excruciating as the chill had been and I quickly retreated to my apartment and locked the door.

I climbed into bed and pulled the covers tightly around my shoulders, but the comfort of my own space offered no refuge.

I spent the rest of the night wide awake, listening for voices and creaking hinges; waiting for the shadows to reappear under my door. But there was only cold and stillness, the same as it had been every night here.

It was only when the first hint of sunlight filtered in through my kitchen window that I finally felt comfortable enough to fall asleep.

5
ARRIVAL

I WAS AWAKENED ONCE AGAIN BY THE SOUND OF footsteps. Unlike the heavy gait that I heard last night, these steps were nimble and energetic. There were voices too. Like the footsteps, they were much different than last night.

"Do you have more stuff coming? Or did you manage to pack everything into these suitcases?"

I immediately recognized the male voice as Philip Barlow's.

"I have some movers coming by later," the girl answered with a polite chuckle. "I don't have a ton of stuff, but it's more than I could've handled by myself."

I assumed that the other voice belonged to

Cassandra Scott. Based on first impressions, she seemed completely normal. But what good were first impressions after what I'd heard last night?

"Understood," Barlow said. "Don't hesitate to let me know if you need any help. If I'm not available, there are plenty of people around to lend a hand. The girl next door to you is named Norah. She's about your age, really nice. She's been here for a while, so she can vouch for how great the place is. Hopefully, you'll get the chance to meet soon."

"I look forward to it," Cassandra said with what sounded like genuine enthusiasm.

I rose out of bed to another sound: the squeaking door of 612, its dry hinges wailing with the same exhaustion as they had last night.

"In the meantime, here are your keys," Barlow continued. "This one allows you to enter the building, this one's for the top lock to the apartment, and this one's for the bottom. It's fine if you make a spare set, just give me a heads-up first."

"Will do."

"Thanks. By the way, I fixed the leak in the kitchen faucet and that little issue with the bedroom window. I meant to come back yesterday to change the bulbs in the fridge, but I got tied up and couldn't make it. I'll bring them by after you've settled in."

"Sounds good. It'll be nice to actually see all the two-dollar frozen dinners I plan to pack the freezer with."

The friendly exchange of laughter did little to quell my sudden anxiety. I'd held out the hope of hearing something that would explain what I experienced last night. But apparently, Barlow hadn't been here before this morning. Neither had Cassandra. So, who did those footsteps belong to? And more importantly, who opened that door?

"Good luck with the rest of your move," Barlow said. "I'll be by later with those bulbs."

The door closed and I heard Barlow grunt softly as he started down the hallway toward the elevator. He grunted the same way when he entered my apartment, and again when he sat on the futon. I couldn't tell if it was the pain of advancing age or some nervous tick that signified the unease of being somewhere he would rather not be. I was leaning heavily toward unease.

I'd convinced myself then that I was

reading too much into the gesture. It was a lot harder to dismiss now.

The elevator chimed upon arriving to pick up Barlow then groaned as its doors closed to take him away. There was complete silence after that. I felt stifled by its suddenness and wanted to blurt out something to break its hold on me.

Instead, I stood there, negotiating a peaceful exit strategy with the ancient reptile inside my brain that told me to run away as fast and as far as I could.

But the logical part of my brain, the part that had functioned exceedingly well before last night, reminded me that there was nothing to run away from. No darkness, no mysterious shadows, no phantom voices. I was safe here. And despite what may have happened elsewhere in the building, I'd always been safe here. Cassandra Scott's presence wasn't going to change that.

Just when I thought that logic had won the negotiation, I heard two faint taps on the living room wall adjacent to 612.

I remembered the detectives, and the thumps inside the walls that followed them around the apartment, and Sullivan's vow to never step foot inside Corona Heights again.

Despite logic's best efforts, I was compelled to run away again.

Then, the reptile inside my brain offered up something else; a thought that wouldn't make sense until much, much later.

Running away won't do any good.

6

SLOW DESCENT

WITH NO CLASSES ON THE SCHEDULE AND A SHIFT AT the café that didn't start until four, I was eager to find something to do outside. I still had my next midterm to study for and decided that a trip to the campus library was the best option.

After a quick shower, I got dressed, grabbed a pre-made salad from the fridge, gathered my backpack and bike, and started for the door. Before reaching it, I stopped, put an ear to the living room wall and listened.

Above the gentle hum of the central heating unit were the sounds of everyday activity. Water from a distant faucet. A zipper being opened and closed. A vibrating cell phone notification. Footsteps gliding gently across the carpet.

What mattered more was what I didn't hear. No husband. No baby. No indication at all that they had ever existed.

Maybe they hadn't existed anywhere but inside my mind. Maybe their presence was nothing more than some lucid dream that my subconscious conjured up as punishment for the darkness that I had exposed it to.

I was tired of grasping at logical explanations that didn't seem to exist. If the entire episode was spawned from a momentary lapse of sanity, I was prepared to live with that. It was certainly better than the alternative.

Momentary insanity.

I silently repeated the phrase until I forced myself to accept the fact that no one was outside my door last night. No one had entered 612 either.

But the dreadful thoughts persisted, and I knew that the only way to keep them at bay was to distance myself from Barlow, Donald Tisdale, and Cassandra Scott's experience in Corona Heights as much as possible. That meant no more stupid research, no more concerns for anyone's safety but my own, and most importantly, no more eavesdropping.

I opened the door as quietly as I could and peered into the hallway. With no sign that anyone was there, I eased my bike past 612 and headed for the elevator. I jabbed at the down button repeatedly until I heard the gears and cables springing to life below. It took nearly a minute of sputtering between floors before it arrived.

As I climbed inside, a door opened somewhere close by. I didn't dare look back, fearing that Cassandra had come out in search of her movers. I knew that I would have to introduce myself eventually, but it was the last thing that I wanted to do right now.

I pressed the 'close' button and backed away from the elevator door. When it didn't move, I hit the button again, and then a third time. Aside from a ping inside the cabin, nothing happened.

Then I heard footsteps.

My panic rising, I jabbed at the button a fourth time. After that, the doors finally drew closed. Despite the persistent sound of approaching footsteps, no one appeared in my increasingly narrow view of the sixth-floor hallway.

Just as I was preparing to breathe a sigh of relief, a frantic voice from the hallway said, "Hold the elevator."

Before I could react, a pale hand appeared between the small opening in the door, preventing it from closing.

When it opened, I saw a short woman with shoulder-length gray hair and gentle, empathetic eyes.

"I'm sorry. I didn't hear you coming," I lied. Now that I realized who was standing next to me in the elevator, I wish that I'd just kept my mouth shut.

What if she can *read minds?* I thought as a winded Iris Matheson turned to me.

"It's fine, sweetheart. My doctor says that I should be taking the stairs anyway." She blew out a loud, long breath and smiled. "I clearly need the exercise."

I felt even worse now. But if I'd honestly known that it was the Ghost Whisperer coming down the hall, would I have done anything differently? It was a fair question. "Again, I'm really sorry."

"Quite alright, young lady," Iris reiterated. "If I want a real workout, maybe I should invest in one of those," she said with a nod to my bike. "Preferably something with a long racing stripe."

When Iris's smile broadened, I smiled back.

I'd only met her a few times since moving in. Once before Donald Tisdale's suicide, and twice after.

I'd heard the rumors about Iris before that. Some people said she was a spirit medium. Others swore that she was a witch. What I mostly saw was a warm, friendly woman with an easy smile and gracious demeanor.

But based on our encounters, I was aware that there was another side to Iris; a side of her that only emerged when she spoke about the building. The soft edges of her tone sharpened, and fear deepened the fine lines in her face.

This energy was the reason why I'd kept our interactions as brief as possible, and why I would go the other way whenever I saw her approaching.

Now, there was no place to go.

I really hope she can't read minds.

"My friend Graham works in a bike shop," I said in an attempt to redirect my thoughts. "I'm sure he can set you up with a good deal,"

"Just what the world needs. Iris Matheson roaming around on two wheels. I'm afraid the roadways aren't wide enough."

She'd managed to disarm me enough to allow another smile to peek through my normally guarded expression.

"First floor?" I asked when I noticed that the elevator still hadn't moved.

"Yes, please."

I pressed the first-floor button and felt a lurch as the cab began its slow descent.

After a short silence, Iris finally said, "Are you headed for class?"

"The library. Big test to study for."

Iris nodded approvingly. "Well, good luck. I'm sure you'll ace it."

"I appreciate the vote of confidence. I'll certainly do my best."

There was a lot to like about Iris, and I felt a sudden twinge of guilt that I'd chosen to judge her so quickly.

"I know you will," she said. "It's a good thing you're going to the library to study. I can imagine that it's been difficult to concentrate around here with all the excitement."

"Excitement?"

"Poor choice of words, I suppose. There's nothing at all exciting about it."

"I still don't know what you mean."

"The new girl moving in next door to you. Cassandra Scott."

My chest suddenly felt tight. "How did you know about that?"

Iris hesitated, as if she were carefully considering her response. "The building talks."

That comment could have been interpreted a million different ways, but I decided that it was in my best interest not to interpret it at all. "Have you met her?"

"No," Iris answered with a hint of disappointment. "I actually came out here hoping to catch a glimpse of her. But I had the pleasure of running into you instead."

She said that last part with enough conviction to make me believe it. "I see."

"What about you?" Iris then asked.

"I haven't met her either. Phillip Barlow swears that the two of us will become best friends. But I've learned to take everything he says with a healthy grain of salt."

"That's very wise of you. I personally

wouldn't trust that man as far as I could throw him." After a moment of reflection, Iris added, "I suppose the feeling is mutual. But that's another story."

I remembered Barlow complaining that certain, unnamed residents had been responsible for creating the building's current reputation, and I wondered now if he was referring to Iris. "I don't think he trusts anyone around here."

Iris's eyes narrowed. "I hope he trusted you enough to be honest about his intentions for moving that girl into 612."

"He told me that he was tired of the rumors about Corona Heights being haunted and he thought that having a tenant in there would help prove that it wasn't true."

Iris shook her head. "Someone needs to have a talk with that girl about what's really going on in here."

Just as I was preparing to ask Iris what that meant, I was interrupted by the ding in the elevator. The doors slid open, revealing the first-floor lobby and a group of teenagers impatiently waiting to board. One of the boys gawked when he saw Iris, but the young girl next to him nudged him in the ribs before he could do anything more.

I slid past them without making eye contact, suddenly feeling self-conscious. If the moment had made Iris uncomfortable, she didn't show it.

Once the kids were inside the elevator, she turned her attention back to me. "Obviously, Barlow doesn't want me talking to Cassandra, not with the way that business from a few months ago has everyone so stirred up."

"You mean the business with Fiona Graves and Hannah Shelby."

"And Donald Tisdale."

I swallowed hard. "So, you believe all of that."

"I saw it with my own eyes, dear. Well, not Donald Tisdale. That was Fiona. But I know she was telling the truth." Iris paused, then asked, "What did you experience during that time?"

"Nothing really. After the police showed up to tell me what happened, I went to my friend Graham's apartment and stayed for a couple of weeks. Fiona once came into the coffee shop where I work to fill out a job application. She seemed really nice. But then Hannah Shelby's stepfather came in and the two of them got into it. Fiona was different after that." I shuddered at the memory. "She stormed out of the shop, and I never saw her again."

"Hopefully she'll never have a reason to come back," Iris said.

"Do you really think it's that bad here?"

"I most certainly do. But Phillip recently put me on notice that I'm not to share that opinion with anyone in the building if I still want a place to live, so, for now, that's just between you and I."

Iris's warm smile did nothing to calm my frayed nerves.

"With any luck, I can meet that young woman before Phillip gets to her," she continued. "If he hasn't already told lies about me, it's only a matter of time before he does."

"Once she meets you, I think she'll know better," I said.

"You're sweet. Maybe you can put in a good word for me when you see her, convince her that I'm not nearly as crazy as everyone seems to think that I am."

Why was I suddenly the one who had to

vouch for everyone's sanity? I could barely manage my own right now.

"I'll see what I can do," I assured her.

But based on the last twenty-four hours, I had strong doubts that I was up to the challenge.

7
THE TALL WEEDS

DESPERATE TO FIND A VOICE OF REASON IN THE growing swell of uncertainty clouding my judgement, I called my classmate and quasi best friend Graham before I left for the library.

"I'm in the tall weeds again," was the answer when Graham asked how I was. That was usually all he needed to hear.

"I'll see you in half an hour."

I reached the campus library in eighteen minutes flat, navigating the downtown streets with expert abandon—avoiding every red light, reckless driver, and clueless pedestrian that I may have otherwise encountered.

Graham was already waiting for me at our

usual table nestled among the stacks of post-Renaissance art books.

He smiled as he pointed to the large cup of coffee waiting on my side of the table.

"Double-shot?" I asked as I took a seat.

"Triple. The call sounded urgent."

"You're such a saint."

"Funny. All the other girls I encounter seem to think so too. Unfortunately, none of them are in the market for saints."

"That's because you're not looking hard enough."

I'd given Graham the proverbial *the right one will eventually come along* speech more times than I could count, but it always fell on deaf ears. I was well aware of my status in his mind as 'the right one' and I was careful to toe the line with his emotions.

He was attractive, in that snarky, intellectually gifted hipster sort of way, but as much as I may have considered it, I knew that it could never be. Graham had been the perfect shoulder to cry on when things got to be too much with my ex, and the role stuck.

"It's my own fault for choosing the most emotionally unavailable girl on the planet," he'd once told me. But I'd silently disagreed with that. There was plenty of emotion left in me. Unfortunately, it wasn't the kind that healthy relationships were built on.

"We can dissect my dysfunctional love life another time," Graham said. "Why don't you tell me what's so urgent? I get the feeling you're not here for an emergency study session."

"There's an issue inside my apartment building."

Graham flashed his snarkiest smile. "You mean spooky central?"

"Yeah," I said with an eye roll.

"Why don't you just move out of that hell-hole already?"

"Because I can't afford to go anywhere else."

"You can stay with me rent-free as long as you need to. I just upgraded to a Queen-sized bed, so there's plenty of room."

"Why do I even bother with you?"

"Because I have all the answers to your sports injury midterm. And I'm charming as hell."

I fought back the involuntary smile that was forming on my face. "Anyway. I'm not moving out."

"Fine. What's the issue?"

"Apartment 612."

Graham's eyes grew wide with intrigue. "Did that old man finally pay you a visit from the grave?"

"I don't think I'll have to worry about that from now on. Someone just moved in."

"No kidding."

"A girl named Cassandra."

"Cassandra, huh? Is she cute?"

"I haven't seen her yet. But I heard her voice this morning. She actually sounds nice."

"Great. So the scary old man will have a nice, and hopefully cute, young girl to keep him company. Where's the problem for you?"

"My landlord wants me to convince her that the building isn't haunted."

Graham laughed hard enough to make me uncomfortable. "But you realize that it *is* haunted, right?"

"I don't know that for sure."

"Are you seriously trying to say that you haven't experienced *anything* in there that makes you think otherwise?"

I heard the baby cooing in my mind as clearly as I heard Graham, but I wasn't quite ready to share that experience—with him or anyone else.

Momentary insanity. That's all it was.

"I'm saying it's not my place to tell that girl anything."

"So why do you feel compelled to?"

"Because my landlord is making me. He's worried that if he can't get more people to move into the building, it'll eventually have to be sold."

"Good. Let it burn to the ground."

"C'mon, Graham. Can you have some empathy for the position I'm in? I could end up on the street if I'm not careful."

Graham's smile went away. "You're right. I'm sorry. What are you going to do?"

"I was planning to avoid Cassandra for as long as I could with the hope that I wouldn't have to say anything. But then I ran into another problem."

"Which is?"

"Iris Matheson."

"You mean that crazy..." Graham began smiling again but quickly pursed his lips to stop it. "That psychic who lives on your floor?"

"Yes. And don't you dare call her crazy again."

Graham threw his hands up in mock deference. "My mistake. What does she have to do with this?"

"I'm afraid that she's going to tell Cassandra her version of the story."

"You mean the truth."

"That's not the point. If Iris does tell her that the building's haunted, and Cassandra ends up going to Phillip Barlow, the whole thing could come down on me."

"So, lie to her and hope that old man Tisdale leaves her alone."

"But what if he doesn't?" The question escaped my mouth before I could stop it.

"Then she could be in a world of shit."

"So could I."

I detected concern in Graham's face for the first time.

"You're overthinking this," he said. "There's a good chance that the topic won't come up at all. And even if it does, Cassandra could be one of those raging agnostics who scoffs at the mere mention of an afterlife. What a fun group they are. Great at dinner parties."

"And if the topic does come up?"

Graham pondered the question for a long

moment. "If she's meant to experience something in there, nothing you can say will make any difference. So, in my opinion, your best bet is to plead ignorance. That way, nothing can be used against you once the crap hits the fan." Graham paused for another long beat. "And if what they say about that 612 is true, the crap *will* hit the fan."

My hand trembled as I reached for the warm coffee cup in front of me.

So much for finding that voice of reason.

8

PLOT TWIST

AFTER TRYING UNSUCCESSFULLY TO SQUEEZE IN some study time after my unsettling conversation with Graham, I eventually made my way back home.

The first thing I saw as I approached the building was the moving truck. It was parked directly in front of the entrance, a long steel ramp sticking out from the back.

I waited at the edge of the parking lot for a long time, hoping to catch a glimpse of anyone coming to or leaving the truck. When I saw no one, I edged closer to get a look inside the back. It was empty except for a large dolly resting on the floor.

"Guess she's all moved in," I said out loud.

Resisting the urge to make a beeline for Graham's apartment and his less than appealing living arrangement, I wheeled my bike through the building's open entryway.

My pulse quickened as I climbed aboard the waiting elevator. I immediately thought about Iris and wondered if she'd already gotten her wish of meeting Cassandra. Part of me hoped that was the case.

Let someone else shoulder the burden of babysitting the newcomer.

But I allowed the thought to pass just as quickly as it came.

Upon exiting the elevator, I was promptly met by two burly men with matching T-shirts that read 'Clive's Moving and Storage'. I was careful to avoid eye contact as I walked past them.

When I rounded the corner, I saw that the door to 612 was partially open.

I paused just long enough to allow for a glance inside. The only thing I saw were two rows of moving boxes stacked in the living room.

I continued the short distance to my own apartment without looking back. I was no more prepared for introductions now then I had been this morning. And after my conversations with Iris and Graham, I may not have been ready at any point in the foreseeable future.

But I knew I couldn't avoid Cassandra Scott forever.

I slid my key into the lock and turned it as gently as I could. The door creaked as it opened. It probably creaked like that every time, but I'd never noticed how loud it was until now. I would have been better off shouting her name at the top of my lungs and getting it over with.

Before I could make it inside, I heard more creaking.

But this time, it wasn't my door.

Instead of moving inside my own apartment, I froze, closed my eyes, and waited for the inevitable moment that would usher in the end of life as I once knew it.

But was it really that dramatic?

"Oh, hey. I thought I heard someone."

It certainly was.

I quickly opened my eyes. By my estimation, I had exactly 0.8 seconds to put on the happiest face that I could.

I turned to my left to see a young, pretty girl standing in the doorway of 612.

To call her pretty would be a drastic understatement. She was stunning, actually, standing a whisker taller than my five-foot seven inches, with long, silky hair the color of chestnuts, wide, alert eyes that shimmered like the world's bluest lagoon, and the lean, perfectly proportioned body of a prima ballerina. It took all the willpower that I had not to duck inside my apartment right then and there, if, for no other reason, than to avoid the harsh glare of Cassandra's radiance.

Instead, I composed myself the best I could, turned on my own smile, which, until now, I thought was pretty darn good, and extended my hand.

"You must be my new neighbor."

"I am," she said, extending her hand in return. "Cassandra. But you can call me Cass if you'd like. It's much easier."

"Hi, Cass. I'm Norah. And... you can call me Norah."

Oh, God. Climb under a rock right now and die.

"Will do, Norah," Cassandra replied with a soft laugh. "It's really nice meeting you."

"Nice meeting you too. I ran into your movers on the way up here. Do you have more things coming?"

"No. They just got the last of it inside. It's not much, but it was more than I could've handled by myself, and since I don't know anyone here, I had to hire Hans and Franz to help me out."

This time, it was me that laughed.

"Their English wasn't very good, but they had arms like tree trunks," Cassandra quipped. "So I figured they'd be up to the challenge."

"From the looks of it, you figured right."

After another exchange of friendly laughter, silence settled between us, and I knew what the next logical question should be. Still, I was hesitant to ask it.

"What do you think about the place so far?"

"I'm really liking the apartment," Cassandra answered. "There's way more space than I'm used to, and it still smells like fresh paint. I'm lucky that I scored such a great deal. There were apartments of comparable size just a couple of blocks away that were twice the price." Something faltered in her face for the briefest of moments that dimmed her bright expression. "But I guess it's not the *perfect* place."

I dreaded responding but knew that I had to. "Do you mean Donald Tisdale?"

Cassandra folded her arms across her stomach as if to cradle it. "Yeah. The building manager told me. It's so awful."

I nodded, unsure of what else to say.

"Did you know him?" Cassandra then asked.

"Not as well as I could have," I answered truthfully. "We had conversations here and there, but he mostly kept to himself. Still, it came as a shock when I heard what happened. He seemed like such a nice man."

"I guess we know that wasn't true," Cassandra said somberly.

"I guess we do," I said, allowing my mind to drift to the dark place that it always had when I thought about Tisdale. "How much do you know about him?"

"Enough that I'd rather not think about it."

"That's understandable," I replied, taking her response as a hopeful sign that the subject wouldn't come up again. "I'm just glad that the apartment is occupied again." Another lie, of course. But it seemed like the right thing to say. "It'll be nice to have some fresh energy around here."

That last part was true. And so far, Cassandra's energy was quite good. It would have to be if Iris and Graham were to be believed.

"I'd like to get the lowdown on the other residents sometime," Cassandra said. "There's bound to be a lot of interesting drama in a place this size."

She didn't know the half of it.

"I try to mind my own business, but I'm sure there are a few helpful tidbits that I can pass along."

The brightness returned to Cass's face. "Sounds like a plan. Are you busy tonight? I still have some things to unpack, but I'd be happy to have you over. I'll spring for pizza and beer, assuming you drink."

"I do."

"Good. It's a date then?"

I was completely caught off guard by the invitation, but the warmth of Cass's presence allowed me to lean into it. "I'm sure you've still got a lot to do in there. I'd be happy to host."

"Excellent. Just give me an hour or so to grab the party favors and I'll head over."

Cass's enthusiasm was contagious, and I was suddenly excited at the prospect of having someone here that I could possibly call a friend.

"I'm looking forward to it."

We ended the conversation with another handshake, then Cass disappeared into her apartment.

Her apartment. Not the infamous 612. Not the fifth most haunted location in the entire state. But a normal place occupied by a normal girl.

A normal girl that I was excited to get to know.

Label this unexpected plot twist number one.

9
THE FOURTH OPTION

THE MORE CASS AND I TALKED, THE MORE IT became clear that we had very little in common.

I was born here. She was born and raised in the Upper East Side of New York City. I was a sports fanatic and marginal student. She was a self-professed drama nerd and voracious reader.

But there was something about our personalities that just clicked. We laughed at a lot of the same things (her sense of humor was as bone-dry as mine), and we both seemed to possess the necessary hard edge that single twenty-something women needed to stay ahead of the world's ever-changing landscape.

It was obvious that we were becoming fast friends, just like Barlow had predicted. Suddenly, I wasn't feeling so slighted by his lack of concern or burdened by his heavy-handed request.

There were still some things that I didn't know, like if Cass was one of those raging agnostics that Graham was so fond of, but with any luck, I'd never have to find out.

"So," Cass said after cracking open her third beer. "On to the building. Any juicy gossip that I should be privy to?"

I'd anticipated this question and had already decided to keep my response as vanilla as possible. "As far as that goes, this place is pretty boring. You have all kinds of people here: young families, retirees, and everything in between. Most people come and go without being a bother to anyone else."

Cass nodded like the response had disappointed her. "Mr. Barlow mentioned that there were a lot of vacancies here, which is surprising given the cheap rent. Do you know what that's about?"

I hadn't anticipated that question and scrambled for an appropriate answer. "I really couldn't tell you. The turnover has always been high here, especially among the younger tenants. They probably just move on to bigger and better things."

"I'd love a house in the suburbs," Cass said dreamily. "White picket fence, big fluffy dog..."

"Husband and 2.5 kids," I added with a smirk.

The gleam in Cass's face dimmed again, more noticeably than it had before.

"Was it something I said?" I asked, sensing her sudden shift.

"It's nothing," she answered unconvincingly. "Just all of the B.S. that we're taught to believe from the time we're born. Perfect families, happy endings, true love, being able to accomplish anything you set your little heart to. It's sad that we're sold lies like that. Endings happen, but in my experience, they're rarely happy."

As much as I agreed with her sentiment, I was thrown by how quickly she went there. I couldn't figure out what I'd said to turn her mood so sour, but I suddenly felt guilty.

"I'm sorry," I blurted out.

Cass blinked, as if my words had snapped her out of a trance, and she was smiling again. "For what? You didn't do anything. I'm the one who drove the conversation off the cliff. I guess my world view is more cynical than it should be sometimes. If it's ever too much, I invite you to call me out on it. You seem like a girl who has her stuff together, and I don't ever want to be counted as a negative influence."

"Trust me, I barely have it together. And I can't see anything about your influence that I would classify as negative. If anything, you're a breath of fresh air that this building desperately needs, and I feel lucky that you ended up here."

This time, I wasn't lying.

Cass responded by raising her bottle. "I could say the same thing about you."

I'd never in been accused of being a breath of fresh air to anyone, but I wasn't in the mood to dissuade her. "Cheers to being lucky."

"Cheers."

After taking a long pull from her bottle, Cass asked, "Do you think I'll feel the same way about the building?"

I swallowed my mouthful of beer with a nervous gulp. This felt like one of those 'rubber meeting the road' kind of moments that can completely change the trajectory of everything that was to follow. I knew the question was coming, of course, but before now, I still hadn't decided how I was going to answer it.

I was being pulled in three different directions: Barlow's denial, Iris's warning, and my own indifference. I knew now that Cass deserved more than indifference, and despite the unexplained things that I'd experienced, I wasn't yet prepared to beat Iris's drum of fear. That left Barlow's denial, which, out of principal, I couldn't fully sign off on either.

So, I created a fourth option, one based more on wishful thinking than substantive evidence.

"I really hope you love it here." Because if she did, maybe I could finally find a reason to love it too.

Cass raised her bottle again and we toasted with all the hope that we could muster.

"Cheers to loving it."

10

1:17 A.M

CASS AND I SEEMED TO LOSE TRACK OF TIME AFTER our toast. There was more beer, more pizza than we could eat, and more conversation, most of it light. I told her about my desire to be the next great Denver Broncos' head trainer, and she shared her dreams of eventually landing a Broadway play. For now, I was a college senior with no immediate job prospects, and she was the new lead in a local production of some family drama penned by a world-famous playwright that I'd never heard of.

By the time the conversation finally dried up, it was late, and we were exhausted. We'd traded in our formal handshakes for sloppy hugs, the way good friends always did after a long night of overindulging, and I watched from my doorway until she made it safely inside her apartment.

Not that there was any danger, I'd told myself half-heartedly. I was simply being overly protective of someone I'd grown quite fond of.

I pulled out my futon without changing out of the sweatshirt and yoga pants that I'd spent the evening in and fell asleep without any notion of what time it was or when I planned to wake up.

I couldn't recall what it was that caused me to jump out of bed. There was no immediate noise that I could detect. But the feeling in my stomach made me believe that I was sinking deep into some void that I wouldn't be able to pull myself out of until I jumped.

So that's what I did.

With my feet on the floor and my head spinning, I turned a bleary eye to the alarm clock.

The neon green jumbled mass slowly took shape until the numbers read 1:17 a.m.

The sinking in my stomach instantly returned and I thought I was going to be sick.

I cradled my stomach to stop it from

churning, then began an unsteady walk to the kitchen for a glass of water. But before I could get there, I was stopped by a muffled voice coming from the other side of the door.

"Shhh. It's okay, princess. This isn't a strange place. We've been here before. Remember?"

In an instant, I felt the full weight of gravity crashing down on top of me. Had I not braced myself against the dinette table, I would have tumbled headfirst unto the floor.

"Come on. Let me know that you remember. She's waited so long to see you again. We don't want to disappoint her."

The infant suddenly began howling with giddy delight.

"Oh, my God," I moaned, my stomach churning violently, my salivary glands preparing my throat for the upturn that my queasy stomach was about to take.

"This can't be happening again."

Still holding on to the table, I directed my disoriented gaze to the sliver of space underneath the door.

The roving shadow from before was there again, moving back and forth, blotting out the light, then allowing it through.

My legs were heavy as I started to walk.

For as frightened as I was to know what was out there, I no longer had only myself to think about.

I hobbled to the door and threw it open, not bothering to check the peephole first.

The hallway was empty, just as I'd somehow suspected it would be.

But I could still hear that otherworldly voice. It was just as terrifying as when I'd first heard it.

Only this time, it wasn't coming from the hallway.

"*What do you say we go to sleep, sweet girl?*"

It was coming from inside Cass's apartment.

"*There, there.*"

The baby began cooing again, and I could hear it being rocked back and forth.

"*We're gonna be just fine here.*"

I quickly approached 612 and put an ear to the door. It was cold to the touch.

"*Do you want to say hi before we go to sleep?*" The voice waited for a response that I couldn't hear. "*Okay. Let's go. I'm sure she'll love the surprise.*"

The next sound I heard was footsteps leading away from the door.

Once the footsteps had disappeared altogether, I ran back inside my apartment and put my ear to the living room wall.

It was completely quiet on the other side.

Then I ran to the bathroom to listen. Still quiet.

I went back into the living room and stood there, unsure of what I'd heard or what I needed to do about it.

My first thought was to knock on Cass's door, but I quickly understood the lunacy of doing such a thing at this time of night with the story I had to tell.

"I was worried that a man and his baby had broken into your apartment so that they could fall sleep next to you."

Instead, I did the only thing I could do. I stood there with my ear to the wall and continued listening.

My legs finally gave out a few hours in and I was forced to get a chair, but I kept my ear to that wall for the entire night.

By the time I heard the first sounds coming from Cass's apartment — a toilet flushing and the subsequent hum of a running faucet — it was 7:25 a.m.

The sun was out, but my apartment felt dark and cold, and I was overwhelmed with that now familiar urge to run away.

Remember, the wary voice in my head warned, *it won't do any good.*

So I didn't move, not even to go to the bathroom.

I couldn't imagine how I looked, but if it was anything like how I felt, I had no business leaving my apartment.

But when I heard the door to 612 opening, that was exactly what I did.

Cass looked rested and alert, despite our late night and the early morning hour.

She was wearing a pair of blue joggers with matching running shoes and a purple fleece.

After adjusting her earbuds, she glanced in my direction.

Her first instinct was to smile. Then she looked closer, and her smile flattened.

"Hey, Norah. Is everything okay?"

"I'm good," I said. But the expression on my face must have told a different story because she seemed unconvinced.

"What's going on?"

I ran a nervous hand through my tousled mess of hair, but I was sure no amount of primping would help at this point. "Nothing much. I heard you come out and I wanted to say hi."

"Oh," she said with an uneasy smile. "Well, hi."

"Are you headed out for a run?"

"Yep. I'm still not completely recovered from last night. That fourth beer was a killer. But I need the air. How are you?"

She gave me a quick once over and I was suddenly self-conscious. "Not at all recovered from last night," I answered with a strained laugh. "But I'll live. I wanted to see how your first night was."

"It was great, all things considered. Totally quiet, just the way I like it."

Even though I fought to keep a neutral expression, I could feel my eyes widening. "That's good. I know that it can take a while to get used to a new place, with all the unfamiliar buzzes and ticks."

"There was none of that," Cass insisted. When I didn't respond, her gaze narrowed. "Are you sure everything's okay?"

Cass's concern was completely justified, but I still felt compelled to downplay it. "Of course. I just have a lot to do today, and I wasn't sure if we'd have the chance to talk later. So I wanted to catch you while I could."

Cass's expression brightened. "That's really sweet of you. I appreciate it."

"Anytime."

"We should get together soon. I'll host this time. Just give me a couple of days to get my apartment together."

"You got it," I said, even though 612 might have been the last place on earth I wanted to be.

"Okay. I'm off then. See you around."

Before I could respond, Cass was making her way to the elevator.

I stood there for a long time after she was gone. I wasn't sure what to make of the exchange, other than the fact that I'd come dangerously close to making a fool of myself.

I couldn't imagine how I'd live this one down in my own mind, but I knew I had to try. It would be easier said than done.

"That bout of insanity may not have been so momentary after all, kiddo."

11

A LIVING, BREATHING THING

I'D MANAGE TO PULL MYSELF TOGETHER LONG enough to make it through a full slate of classes and a short shift at the cafe. I spent half the day thinking about Graham's offer to stay at his apartment (which was becoming more tempting by the hour), and the other half worrying that my stunt with Cassandra this morning may have cost me a much-needed friendship.

What I didn't think about was that voice.

Or that baby.

Or the fact that I was quite possibly losing my mind.

I couldn't decide which prospect was

scarier: the voices being real or the voices being figments of my overwrought imagination.

There would be a reckoning either way. But I couldn't bear to consider that right now.

I left work with the intention of grabbing some grossly unhealthy takeout, scrolling my online feed until I stumbled across a cute cat video that I could watch twenty times (it filled the void left by the building's ridiculous 'no pet' policy), and zoning out until there was nothing left in my mind but empty space.

When I entered the building at the precise moment that Iris Matheson was exiting the elevator, I knew that the Universe had a different plan in store.

Iris smiled the instant she saw me. It was one of those warm, motherly smiles that instantly made you feel comfortable. I hadn't always felt that way when I saw Iris. But I did now.

She must know that you need it, I thought, wondering if she heard me.

"Hi, Norah," she said as she sat down the laundry basket that she'd been carrying.

"How are you, Iris?"

"Better now that I've seen a friendly face."

I couldn't help but smile back.

"It's funny that I should run into you," she continued. "I'd been wondering if you'd gotten the chance to meet Cassandra yet."

"I did. We had dinner last night. She's a really nice girl who seems to have her head on straight."

Unlike someone else I know.

"That's wonderful. And did you get a sense of how her first night went?"

It was shitty for me. In case you were wondering.

"Just fine from what she said."

Iris nodded. "I'm relieved to hear that. Let's hope it stays that way."

That last statement caught my attention. "Are you worried that it won't."

Iris hesitated before responding. "I worry about a lot of things. Too many things if I'm being honest."

"Is there something about 612 in particular that worries you?"

"It shouldn't be occupied," Iris said without blinking. "And Phillip Barlow had no business pushing the issue."

I heard that voice again.

"*We're finally here, princess.*"

"What really happened in there?"

Iris looked around as if she were concerned that someone else was listening. "It's not in my best interest to talk about it as long as that man is anywhere around. He's made that abundantly clear."

"Does he think that you're the one who spread the rumor about the building?"

"That it's haunted?"

I nodded.

"I'm sure he thinks it's me. But this place also has a voice. And it can speak on its own behalf loud and clear." Iris paused. "Still, Phillip thinks that I'm a dangerous influence."

"Because of what you know."

"Because of what I've seen. Because of what I fear may still be happening here."

"In 612?"

"Not just there."

"But 612 is part of it."

Iris hesitated again before nodding.

"Do you think that Cass is in danger?"

"I suppose that depends on her and what she's bringing with her."

"Meaning?"

"Her state of mind. Corona Heights is like a sponge. It absorbs the energy of everything around it. And it responds to some energies more than others.

She was speaking about the building like it was a living, breathing thing, and suddenly, I was reminded of why I preferred to go the other way when I saw her coming. "What kind of energy?"

"Dark energy. Pain. Sadness. Guilt. That energy is the most powerful, and unfortunately, the most pervasive, at least here. Some of us are able to remain relatively unscathed because we don't embody that darkness. But others, usually through no fault of their own, aren't so lucky. Time will tell which of those camps that Cassandra falls into. I hope it's as you say. But if it's not..."

"What?"

"It sounds like the two of you spent a fair amount of time together, so you may have some idea of what her baseline personality is. Watch for any abrupt changes. If something is going on in there, and I pray that there isn't, that change could occur very quickly."

I felt an icy current of fear streaking up my

back. "I have to admit, you're scaring me with this."

Iris nodded and cast her eyes to the floor. "I was warned against doing that. I didn't mean to, sweetheart. I just want you to stay alert."

"And what am I supposed to do if I notice a change in her? Tell Phillip Barlow?"

"That's the last thing you should do, Norah. My door, on the other hand, is always open. Promise me you'll use it if you need to."

Right now, I wasn't sure if that prospect was any better than telling Barlow. But there was something about Iris that made me want to trust her. "I promise."

Iris nodded, then said, "I guess I should ask how you've been through all of this change? Is everything okay?"

Instead of the man's voice, I heard the baby this time.

"Between school and work, I'm just trying to keep my head above water."

I'd wanted to lie outright and tell her that everything was fine. But if she was as insightful as I thought she was, I knew that she'd see right through it.

Iris nodded at my response, but as I'd feared, her eyes told me that she knew more.

"I'm here anytime you need me. And I'm easy to reach."

Somehow, I knew exactly what she meant. Just like I knew that I would be taking her up on that offer. Very soon.

12

A BONA FIDE MYSTERY

I WASN'T IN THE MOOD FOR UNHEALTHY TAKEOUT OR adorable cat videos by the time I got back to my apartment. I instead found myself preoccupied with the activity inside 612, or should I say, the lack of activity.

It wasn't quite seven yet, so it was entirely possible that Cass was still out, griding away at a late rehearsal or familiarizing herself with the city. The quiet was unsettling, given the conversation I'd just had with Iris and my own experience last night.

A silent 612 could have meant so many things right now. But all the scenarios I imagined were really bad.

I thought about Detective Sullivan and the

thumping in the walls and ceiling. Then I made the mistake of conjuring an image of what could have caused that thumping.

Bad idea.

Corona Heights is like an energy sponge. A living, breathing thing. A parasite.

I turned away from the dreadful thought, suddenly hyperaware of my own energy.

I wasn't the keeper of any secrets. Not conscious ones, anyway. Aside from an especially nasty break up six months ago, my life was as mundane and predictable as they came. There were no earth-shattering tragedies staining my life. I'd never been in any real physical danger. Both my parents were still alive and well (though, they'd chosen to move more than a thousand miles away upon my high school graduation—did they secretly hate me or something?). And I have a fairly healthy relationship with alcohol and other legally available mind-altering substances.

According to Iris's logic, I should have been just fine here.

But as I nervously paced my apartment, awaiting some imaginary hammer to fall on my head, I felt anything but fine.

I wasn't sure what that hammer was for

the longest time. But, like the *thing* in the pit of my stomach, that nightmare that wasn't ending nearly as swiftly as I would have liked, the answer revealed itself with a knock on the door.

Unable to trust anything I heard now, I cautiously approached before putting my eye to the peephole.

Cass was smiling that ever-radiant smile when I opened the door.

"Hey, neighbor."

"Hey, Cass." I managed a smile of my own, despite the nauseating stir inside my stomach. "How are you?"

"I'm great," she said with all the certainty that could come with making such a statement. "Are you busy?"

"Not really. What's up?"

"Would you like to come over? I got my place together in record time and I'd love for you to see it."

"Now?"

"If that's okay."

I looked back in my apartment and pointed a thumb to some imaginary project inside that suddenly couldn't wait. "I would, but I'm kind of..."

"Can I entice you with wine, at least? I promise, I won't keep you."

Despite the vehement protest from the ancient reptile inside my brain, I couldn't say no, especially after this morning. I needed a chance to redeem myself.

"Sure. Let's go."

Cass's apartment, the infamous 612, was much brighter and more inviting than I'd expected.

The walls were a crisp eggshell white and looked to be freshly painted. There were appliances in the kitchen that were at least a decade newer than mine (I'd have to talk to Barlow about that), and the decor was warm and homey, with artful renderings of classic Hollywood starlets on the walls, a plush leather sofa and matching recliner, and a colorful array of candles that undoubtedly smelled amazing.

"Wow," was all I could manage. "What a place."

Cass smiled modestly. "When Barlow told me what happened in here—the previous tenant's suicide—I felt like I needed to overcompensate."

"I'd say it's just right."

"I'm happy to hear that. Do you mind if I show you the rest before we crack open that bottle?"

"Lead the way," I said before taking my first real step inside.

After that, everything changed.

The air suddenly felt thin, and I found myself inhaling through my mouth to catch my breath. The churning inside my stomach that had subsided was now back and much more deliberate in its attempts to handicap me.

Then I began recalling the scant details that floated around the building regarding Tisdale's suicide.

The recliner he stood on.

The utility hook he drilled into the doorframe.

The thick braided rope that he used to end his life.

Hannah Shelby's vengeful ghost forcing him to do it.

That last one was mere conjecture on the part of the gossip mongers in the building, and Iris never confirmed it.

But I could vividly imagine it just the same.

Cass led me through a short hallway lined with more classic movie posters until we entered her bedroom.

"I'm even more jealous now," I said with a hard swallow as she flicked the light on. "I'd have given anything to land a one-bedroom here, but they were all occupied when I moved in. Now, they're too expensive."

I had the thought that the acting business must have been good for Cass to afford one. I wanted to ask about it, but it didn't feel right under the circumstances.

"I'm so lucky to have found it," Cass said. "I about died when I saw the closet."

She pushed open the sliding door to reveal a tidy hanging wardrobe and rows of shoeboxes lined neatly on the floor.

"At the risk of making you even more jealous, come have a look."

I thought about the trapdoor that just *appeared out of nowhere* and worried that it would pop up again, undetected, and swallow Cass and I whole.

I thought about the mysterious pool of blood in the corner and worried that ours would be the next to spill.

I thought about running. Far, far away.

Damn it, I said it won't do any good!

"I can see it just fine from here," I said from my anchored spot near the door. "Amazing."

"Thanks. I'm so glad you like it. You're the first one to see it. Knowing my luck, you'll be the *only* one to see it for quite some time."

"Come on. A gorgeous girl like you probably has boys on both coasts lining up for your attention."

Cass's face dropped without warning. I wasn't exactly sure what a forlorn expression actually looked like, but the dull emptiness in her eyes was what I imagined.

"I'm not really in the market."

I smiled as brightly as I could to maintain the buoyant energy that Cass had established. "I can imagine that you're busy with the play and all the rehearsals. My own work life balance sucks like all hell. That's the excuse I use to explain my crappy dating life anyway."

"It's not that," Cass said in a faraway voice that sounded like something out of a hazy dream.

Then, as quickly as she fell under the spell of a distant, yet easily accessible memory, she snapped out of it. "Anyway, I did find something interesting in the closet as I was moving in."

"Oh yeah? What was it?"

"These."

She retrieved a pair of eyeglasses from atop her chest of drawers. When I looked closer, the frame appeared to be cracked down the middle and one of the lenses was missing.

"That is interesting," was all I could think to say.

"Yeah. My first thought was that they belonged to Mr. Barlow or someone renovating the apartment. But they looked small enough to fit a young kid. So, I asked him if he had a child or grandchild who could've left them behind. He swore he'd never seen them."

"Sounds like a bona fide mystery," I said, leaving it at that.

"Yeah." She put the glasses back on the chest. "I should throw them away. It's doubtful the owner is coming back."

Let's hope they don't.

"What do you say we have some wine?" Cass said. "We'll make a housewarming out of it."

"Sounds good," I said as I gave the bedroom one final scan. It was then that I noticed the pictures on the nightstand.

And the display frame hanging over the bed.

It was also then that I felt every drop of the life-force that kept me upright begin to drain from my body.

I stared at the frame long enough for Cass to notice.

That forlorn look, far beyond sadness, returned to her face shortly afterward.

"Those were Claire's."

I stood there in frozen silence waiting for her to elaborate.

"My baby."

"Did you say they *were* Claire's?"

Cass nodded, and I could see the delicate structure that held her face together crumbling in real time.

"I'm so sorry."

"Her father and I were planning to get married. She was eight months old. Too small to be a flower girl, of course. But we got her the cutest little pink dress."

I imagined it matching the pink mittens and beanie that were displayed in the frame.

The structure in my face wasn't nearly as deli-cate as Cass's, but I nearly lost it just the same.

"We'd just found a florist," she continued. "She and Adam were driving to meet me there, when..."

I'd never been more grateful for an unfin-ished sentence.

After taking a long moment to compose herself, Cass said, "There's not a day that goes by that I don't wish I was with them, wherever they are. There's no word to describe the void inside of me. I try to fill it with healthy things. But then I hear them. Adam and my little princess, begging me to be with them."

Princess. Oh God.

"Their voices are only in my head. I know that. But sometimes, I'll sit in silence for hours so those made-up voices can play in my mind over and over again."

Tears shot out of Cass's eyes and landed in powerful bursts on her cheek and blouse.

She wiped them away with her bare hand, but they kept coming.

"Let me get you some tissue," I said with one foot already pointed to the bathroom.

"That's okay. I like the way they feel. And they're a reminder that I need to feel something beyond this numb detachment. I'll be okay."

"Are you sure?" I said, doubting her.

"No," she quickly admitted. "I don't know what it is, but ever since I've been here, the pain is just so present. Like it's sitting on top of my chest." Cass paused. "A month after the accident, I tried to kill myself. Two weeks later, I tried again. Obviously, I didn't succeed. After time and a lot of therapy, I came to think that I was here for a reason. And there were moments when I whole-heartedly believed it. But the pain I'm feeling now... it's as raw as the moment I got that phone call. And I really need it to go away."

"Cass, I'm so sorry." I took a step toward her, but she put her hands up to stop me.

"Don't, Norah. It's okay. As much as I'd like it to stop, I need to feel this. I need to feel... *something*."

No longer recognizing the girl standing in front of me, I slowly backed away until I was nearly out the bedroom door. "Are you sure you don't need anything?"

"I'm sure," she said in that faraway voice. "I'm sorry, but I think you should go."

"I'd like to stick around for a while if it's all the same, just to make sure—"

"I said no," Cass repeated. But her pleading eyes were saying something else. "I prefer to be alone when I get like this. I'll sort it out."

"Are you sure?" I said with a pleading gaze of my own. "It's not a problem."

"It is for me."

The desperation in Cass's eyes disappeared in that moment. There was something cold and unfeeling in them now.

"Okay," I finally relented. "As long as you're—"

"Let's just plan to do this another time, alright?"

I was pushed back on my heels by the raw anger in her voice. "No problem. I'll show myself out."

When I did, Cass didn't follow.

13
AN EMOTIONAL SCENE

I STAYED UP FOR A GOOD PORTION OF THE NIGHT with my ear to the wall of Cass's apartment. I felt guilty for eavesdropping, especially because I promised myself that I wouldn't. But it was the only thing I could do to ensure that she was okay.

Aside from a few muted sniffles late last night and early this morning, all was quiet. Easier to replay those made-up words in her mind, I supposed.

They were likely the same words that I was once certain had been created in my own mind.

"I'm sure she misses you, princess."

I knew for a fact that she did.

The question I feared asking was: "How far is Cass willing to go to see her?"

So far, this was playing out exactly as Iris thought it would.

"This place feeds off of dark energy."

"When the change happens, it will be quick."

Considering what I'd experienced in my apartment, and my time in 612 last night, I'd learned not to doubt anything that Iris said. But I wasn't prepared for how frighteningly accurate she would be. Or how quickly I'd need to accept her invitation.

"I'm here anytime you need me And I'm easy to reach."

I really hoped that was true.

I'd just walked out of the bathroom where I was struggling in vain to make myself presentable when I heard Cass's voice coming through the wall.

"You deserved everything that happened, you fucking asshole. *I* would kill you if I could. Ten times over! You had no business leaving me. You took everything from me, you irresponsible prick. *Everything!*"

I was shocked, mortified, and saddened all at once by what I was hearing.

If Iris herself had told me that Cass could

fall into the darkness of her agony this far, this fast, I never would have believed it.

And even now, hearing it with my own ears, I still couldn't believe it.

"I'm tired of being the one made to pay for what *you* did. Do you understand? I'm not paying anymore!"

After Cass's last frantic cry, I ran outside and began pounding on her door. I decided that I'd only give her a few seconds to answer. With Barlow's apartment on the first floor and no one else near us, it would be up to me to kick the door in.

You don't do all those squats for nothing, girl.

Thankfully, Cass answered right away. Her eyes were stained red and nearly swollen shut with the crippling residue of unchecked emotion, yet she seemed completely perplexed by my presence.

"Are you okay, Cass? I could hear you all the way in my apartment!"

She met my frantic greeting with a look that I couldn't quite interpret. It may have been irritation; it could have been scorn. It certainly wasn't an invitation to stay.

"I'm sorry I was so loud," she said flatly. "I was running lines." She held up the script for good measure. "It's an emotional scene and I guess I got into character a little too deeply. Method acting at its finest."

Her smile was as flat as her voice, and I feared that the sweet, bubbly girl that I'd met just two nights ago was either a clever facade or was overtaken by whatever else had resided in there with her.

I knew which option Iris would choose.

"I'm sorry I bothered you."

"I'm sorry I was so loud. I should have warned you."

"It's okay," I said with a thin smile. "I'll just consider this my warning."

Cass sent me away with a heartless shrug as she closed the door in my face.

14

THE BOOGEYMAN

Unlike Cass, Iris didn't look the least bit perplexed to see me. Unfortunately, her beaming enthusiasm disappeared the instant she looked into my eyes.

"Uh-oh. This doesn't feel like a social visit."

"I'm worried about Cass."

Iris nodded before gently taking me by the arm. "Come in, sweetheart."

The gravity of the moment hadn't allowed me to focus on much of her apartment, aside from the picture of a man I presumed was her husband on proud display near the door.

The space was warm in a soothing way,

and my nostrils were filled with the intoxicating aroma of cinnamon and spice. It made me want to stay much longer than I knew I could.

"Would you like anything to drink?" Iris asked in the way that all perfect hosts did.

"No, thanks. This is kind of urgent."

"I gathered. But you're shaking like a leaf, and you need something to help regulate your breathing. Perhaps some tea."

I took in the deepest breath that I could and let it out slowly until I felt my racing heart begin to calm. "I'm good now. I promise."

Iris looked me up and down before saying, "Okay. So, what's this business with Cassandra?"

"You asked me to be on the lookout for any changes in her baseline behavior."

"That's right. And did you notice anything?"

"More things than I could count."

I then proceeded to tell her everything about my visit last night, and our bizarre encounter this morning. I conveniently left out my own possible turn with the supernatural.

After Iris took some time to absorb the story, she said, "And the glasses that she found in the closet. Were the frames cracked in the center?"

I was almost relieved by the question. She knew what she was doing, and I desperately needed that. "Yes."

"And were they small enough to fit a child?"

"Yes."

Iris was silent for a moment, as if she were hesitant to reveal the information that needed to come next. "They belonged to Hannah Shelby."

I was surprised by my lack of surprise.

"Did she find anything else?" Iris asked before I could respond.

"Not that she mentioned. What's in that apartment, Iris?"

"Ugly things, potentially."

"Then we have to warn her."

"Not yet. We don't know enough."

"What else is there to know?"

I knew there was little I could do to win this argument without sharing my own experience.

"Why don't you tell me," Iris said.

Despite the pointedness of her question, I couldn't.

"I've already told you what I know."

Iris took another long moment to process my lie. Then she said, "Maybe I could go over there and introduce myself."

"That's a good idea. I'd like to come too."

Iris shook her head. "I'd prefer to go alone. This time, at least. I just baked some cookies last night and I can bring them as a welcome gift. She won't suspect anything else. But with you there, she might."

I couldn't deny the logic. "Can I at least eavesdrop from my apartment?"

Iris's kind smile returned. "Knock yourself out, kid."

I was relieved to hear that. I'd become quite adept at listening in on the lives of other people, in this realm and, apparently, the one beyond.

"Just give me a second to grab those cookies and we'll be on our way," Iris said.

My pulse rose with each brisk step that we took to Apartment 612. I was too nervous to stand, and I wasn't even going in there. I felt a stirring of gratitude for Iris's wisdom in keeping me away and my own for not lodging a protest.

Just as 612 finally came into view, I heard the ding of the arriving elevator.

I didn't think that anything frightened Iris. But when I saw the abject terror on her face with the appearance of Phillip Barlow, I was reminded that boogeymen came in all stripes and persuasions.

He looked at me first, presumably, to get the phony smile out of the way. "Hey there, Norah."

"Hi, Mr. Barlow," I replied with the stiffest poker face that I could summon.

"I told you before that Phillip will do just fine."

"Yes, Norah. Phillip suits him much better."

Barlow rolled his eyes at Iris before turning back to me. "Where are you two headed with those delicious treats?"

I blurted out, "We're going..." before Iris wisely cut me off.

"Norah was kind enough to help me with some groceries today and I was repaying her with these. No crime in gratitude, right?"

"Funny. I didn't see you downstairs."

"Funny. I didn't realize that you were keeping tabs on me."

Embarrassment overtook Barlow's gruff face, and he turned his attention back to me. "As long as that's all it is."

"What else would it be?" I asked him with a stab of defiance.

"Yes, Phillip. What else would it be?"

Barlow looked at her with eyes that said "You know *exactly* what I mean" before he turned a quick glance toward 612. "Just making sure everyone's happy."

"We're thrilled, Phillip," Iris responded with a stone-faced snarl. "Can't you tell?"

Barlow drew in a nervous breath and nodded. "Right. Well, enjoy those cookies, Norah."

"I will, Mr. Barlow."

"Wonderful. Maybe you can share them with Cassandra Scott. I take it you two have met."

"We have."

"And did you become fast friends like I predicted?"

"We're thick as thieves already."

Barlow looked pleased. "I'm counting on you to take care of her, at least until she gets properly situated."

"She's a big girl, Phillip. I'm sure she's perfectly capable of taking care of herself."

He ignored Iris and kept his white-hot glare on me. "You never know from which direction the bad influences will come from around here."

Barlow didn't take the time to explain what that meant, and Iris didn't bother asking. We simply let him slither down the hall in silence until he was gone.

I turned to Iris with a look of concern that felt entirely appropriate. "Maybe you should save the introductions for another time."

If Iris shared my concerns about Barlow, she was good at not showing it. "Agreed."

I turned a dubious eye to Cass's door. "What should I do in the meantime?"

"Keep an eye on her. I'll pay a visit as soon as I can."

With the way things were going, I had a sinking feeling that neither Cass nor I would be around long enough to see that happen.

Ridiculous, the logical part of my brain said.

Hardly, the ancient reptile coyly responded.

I took Iris's cookies and watched her amble down the hall.

My growling stomach couldn't wait to devour them.

But I'd be sure to save a few for Cass. Just in case I was wrong.

15
STRANGE THINGS

THE REST OF THAT NIGHT AND THE FOLLOWING morning hummed along without incident.

Cass had appeared to run out of lines to rehearse (if that's what she was really doing), and the muted sounds I heard now were more of the everyday variety that I'd expected.

I was in the middle of my shift at the cafe, mindlessly watching the steamed milk from someone's specialty mocha latte overflow onto the countertop, when Cass walked in.

In the drunken haze of our first meeting, I couldn't remember if I told her where I worked. But based on the look of quiet determination on her face, I assumed that she was here for me.

I gave the customer his hastily made mocha, waiting patiently for a complaint that, thankfully, didn't come, before I approached Cass from behind the counter.

"Hey, you," I said with my most authentic City Perk Cafe cheeriness. "What sounds good today?"

"An apology from me," she replied. "Do you have a minute to talk?"

"Only if you order something first," I said in an attempt to lighten the mood. "The triple strawberry rhino horn smoothie is all the rage right now."

She didn't bite at the humor. "I'll take a small light roast. No cream, no sugar."

"Sounds perfect."

After fetching Cass's coffee, I was able to sneak away with her to a table in the back.

Her eyes were still red and puffy, like she hadn't stopped crying, and her body was rigid with tension.

"I just wanted to say that I'm sorry for last night," she began. "And also, for this morning. One of the reasons why I enjoy acting so much is that it allows me to express my emotion through other people and their experiences. I can transfer all my baggage to them. It was the one thing that helped me get through the grief in the beginning. Sometimes, I think I still rely too much on it. This morning was one of those times."

"I understand, Cass. And I'm sorry that you had to relive all of that. If I did anything to make it worse—"

"You didn't," Cass insisted. "The pain is always there. It doesn't take much to bring it to the surface."

"And you say that it's gotten worse since you moved into Corona Heights?"

"A lot of things have gotten worse since I moved in."

"Like what?"

Cass paused like she was mentally itemizing the list in order of importance. Finally, she said, "Do you ever experience strange things in there?"

"Strange things?" I said, knowing full well what she meant.

"I don't know how to describe it beyond that. Nothing feels right. I sensed it the very first day, even before I met you."

"It's a new place" I said. "And considering what happened in there..."

"I'd like to show you something. Can you come over later?"

I couldn't bear the thought of being in that apartment again, not without Iris. There was something bad in there. I was convinced of that now. But I couldn't say no, not when Cass was this desperate. "Of course."

You had your chance to run, the ancient reptile in my head scoffed. *It's too late now.*

16

AN ADMISSION OF GUILT

I MADE IT TO CASS'S APARTMENT A FEW HOURS later. She opened the door without saying anything and promptly led me to her bedroom. She didn't speak until she walked inside the closet.

"Do you remember the glasses I showed you last night?"

How could I possibly forget? "Yes."

"I finally got around the throwing them away after you left." Cass bent down to pick up something off the closet floor. "This morning, I found these." She presented the glasses. Same cracked frame. Same missing lens.

"Where?"

"On the floor, in the exact spot where I'd found them the first time."

I didn't know what to say, so I didn't say anything.

"But that wasn't the worst of it," Cass continued. She bent down again. When I saw what was in her hand this time, I let out an audible gasp.

The thick rope was tightly knotted in the front, with a large loop just big enough for...

"Where did that come from?" I asked.

Cass tightened her grip on the rope like she had no intention of letting go. "I think it belongs to the apartment," she said matter-of-factly. "I guess it wants me to have it now."

I didn't like where this was going. "Cass..."

"But wait," she interrupted. "This is the best part." She walked over to the frame that displayed the mittens and beanie.

I hadn't noticed the large crack in the center until Cass pointed it out.

"This happened last night too. Sometime after you left."

"Did it fall?" I asked stupidly. Right now, I needed to grasp at anything I could.

"No, it didn't."

Cass dropped the rope on the bed and

walked toward me. "Do you know what's happening to me?"

I fought the urge to back out of the room. "Cass... I..."

"Tell me the truth, Norah. Do you know why this is happening? Has something like this happened to you too?"

I suddenly thought about that voice.

Adam.

And that baby,

Claire.

The princess.

After that, I couldn't lie anymore.

"I started hearing things the night before you moved in."

"What kinds of things?"

"Voices. A man and... a baby."

The delicate structure holding Cass's face together completely collapsed this time. "What do you mean?"

"I tried to dismiss it the first time. But then I heard it again, coming from your apartment. That's why I came over that morning. I wanted to make sure you were okay."

"You heard a man and a baby in my apartment, and you didn't think to tell me?"

"I didn't want to scare you. You'd just

moved in, and you seemed so happy, and Phillip Barlow wanted to make sure that you weren't..." I stopped myself.

"What, Norah?"

"He wanted to make sure that you weren't negatively influenced by what some people say about the building."

"What do they say?"

You had your chance to run.

"That it's haunted."

Cass bit down on her lip, perhaps to stop herself from saying something that she didn't want to. Not that I didn't deserve it.

"So, Mr. Barlow lied to me, and he recruited you to lie too?"

"It's not that simple, Cass."

"Yes, it is."

"I didn't believe any of the talk about this place being haunted. Even when I heard those voices. I thought it was all in my head. But when I came over here last night and saw that frame, and I heard you refer to Claire as princess..."

Cass's eyes narrowed in anger. "What about that?"

"The voice I heard—the male one—referred to the baby as princess."

Cass began shaking her head furiously. Her eyes were wide with rage. "You're lying."

"I'm not."

"Yes, you are. Why would they come to you and not..."

"It's the building, Cass. It's not them."

Cass wrapped her arms around her narrow waist and began pacing the room. "No."

"There's someone who can explain it to you a lot better than I can. Her name is Iris, and she's a psychic medium. She knows what's going on here and she can help you."

"I don't want her help. I want my baby."

"Cass, that wasn't your baby."

She stopped pacing and took dead aim at me. "Why do you keep saying that?"

"Because I'm afraid it's true. This place can really screw with your mind if you allow it to. The glasses. The rope. The broken frame. Those voices. You have to see the connection."

"I see, alright," Cass answered before turning her dead eyes to the frame. "I see that you're all a bunch of liars." When Cass turned back to me, her bottom lip was quivering. "And you're the worst of them."

That one felt like a baseball bat to the

chest. "Cass, can you please talk to Iris? I know she can—"

"I don't want to talk to her. I don't want to talk to you either."

Without saying another word, Cass stormed out of the bedroom. I had to force my heavy legs to follow.

She opened the door, then stepped aside.

I walked into the hallway then turned back. "It could've all been in my head, Cass."

"It wasn't. You know that. So, stop lying to me."

"Cass, if you just—"

"Goodbye, Norah."

She slammed the door in my face before I could respond.

17
CRUDE THREATS

I'D BEEN SITTING ON THE COUCH FOR WELL OVER AN hour, unsure of what to do next, when there was a knock on my door.

I leapt to my feet, thinking that it was Cass. I wasn't sure what was left to say, but after what I'd done, I owed her the courtesy of listening.

I opened the door without looking to see who was on the other side.

When I saw the look on Phillip Barlow's face, I immediately realized my mistake.

"Hi, Mr. Barlow."

"Spare me the hollow greeting. I asked you to do one simple thing."

"I don't know what you—"

"Cassandra Scott just left my apartment in tears, calling me a liar, saying that you and I conspired to keep the truth about this building from her. Where would she get such an idea, Norah?"

"Mr. Barlow..."

"She even threw in Iris Matheson's name for good measure. Said that you wanted the two of them to meet so they could figure out what was wrong with her apartment." Barlow paused to refill his anger tank. "There's *nothing* wrong with her apartment."

"Yes, there is."

Barlow and I jumped simultaneously at the new voice.

I hadn't noticed that Iris was there until she peered around Barlow's broad shoulder. To say that I was relieved to see her would be the understatement of the millennium.

Barlow turned to her with eyes that were stoked with fury. "Why are you here, Iris?"

"To try and talk some sense into you."

"Damn it, we've been through this already. I thought you and I had come to an understanding?"

"That changed the instant you allowed someone to move into that apartment. You know what happened in there. You know what Fiona Graves experienced. You know the hell those two little girls went through. You should've boarded that place up. Instead, you essentially forced a vulnerable girl to move in. What good did you think would come from that?"

"I don't have time for this. I have to go straighten things out with that young woman before she ends up suing us for emotional distress." He looked at Iris, then at me. "And if that happens, I'll make sure the two of you are at the defendant table right along with me."

Before Iris or I could respond to Barlow's crude threat, we were startled by another voice.

"Shut up, you bastard! Don't you dare try and talk me out of this. What, you don't think I'll do it? The rope is right here. I can end it all right now. Just like that!"

The three of us descended on the door in an instant.

Cass answered Barlow's heavy-handed knock answered right away.

The first thing I saw were her eyes. They were that blood shot, puffy mess of emotion that I'd sadly gotten used to seeing.

The next thing I noticed was the script.

"What do you want?"

"We heard some commotion over here," Barlow stammered. "Are you okay?"

She lifted the script. "I'm rehearsing."

Barlow didn't know what to say to that, so he looked at me.

"Cass, I'm really sorry that—"

"Can you please leave me alone? It's almost time and I need to finish prepping."

Almost time for what? I wanted to ask.

As I looked deeper into her eyes, I realized that there was nothing left of the girl I'd first met. I felt a large knot in my throat that I struggled to swallow.

"Of course," Barlow said. "If you need anything..."

Cass responded by closing the door in his face.

He turned to Iris and me with venomous eyes. "I hope you're happy."

"Far from it," Iris said. "That girl needs help, Phillip. Shame on you for not seeing it."

"And shame on you for breaking your word." Barlow turned to me. "Both of you. Leave Cassandra alone. I mean it." He stood in front of the apartment like he planned to guard it for the rest of his life.

Iris looked at me, then turned to Barlow before starting down the hallway. "I hope you don't live to regret this."

Barlow crossed his arms and stuck out his chest, fortified in his new role as Cass's guardian.

"I'm sorry," Iris then said to me.

"Me too."

When I turned to back Barlow, he could only shake his head.

18

LAYING THE TRAP

IT WAS LATE WHEN I HEARD A GENTLE TAP ON MY door, followed by the sound of Cass's voice.

"Norah? Are you here?"

I begrudgingly rose from the futon. Even though I was sure it was her, I still looked through the peephole. I'd had enough nasty surprises for one day.

I opened the door and immediately took a step back.

The person I saw standing in front of me looked like Cass, but it wasn't her. Her eyes were dull and listless. Her porcelain skin was ashen. Her hair, once long and silky, was now matted and tangled.

"I finally figured it out."

When she smiled, I saw something that scared me.

"Do you want to know what it is?"

My first instinct was to close the door, but she stepped in front of it before I could.

I pushed hard against her, employing every muscle I'd developed through my years of working out. But I was no match against her strength.

Where had that strength come from?

She was on top of me before I could come up with an answer.

"I figured out that you're trying to take them away from me."

Cass was pressing down on my chest, and it was hard to breathe. I tried to scream, but she put a cold, heavy hand over my mouth, clamping it shut.

"But I won't let you. And neither will he."

The last thing I felt was something cool and very hard striking me in the face.

19
MONSTER

THE FIRST IMAGE I SAW WHEN I REGAINED consciousness was a popcorn ceiling, gleaming with a fresh coat of white paint. I knew then that I wasn't in my apartment.

When I tried to lift my head, I felt something choking me. When I attempted to relieve the pressure, I realized that my wrists were bound together.

When I heard Cass's voice, I knew exactly where I was.

"I thought it was me that had to die in order to be with them again. But he told me the truth."

I tried to move my legs, but they were

bound too. Pain shot through my body in cascading waves.

"He told me that you had to die. Right here, where he died. He sacrificed himself as an offering to this place, this evil, ugly place. And now, it needs another. He promised that Adam and Claire were here, waiting for me. And we'll all get what we want, thanks to your sacrifice."

"Cass, please don't do this." My voice was hoarse and muffled. She'd put something over my mouth.

"You thought you were going to claim them without me ever finding out. But he saw to it that I found out. He's the only one who understands. Not you. Not Barlow. Not that fucking psychic. He's in pain, just like I am. And together, we're going to make that pain go away."

The only thing I felt beyond my physical distress were the warm tears streaking down my temples.

"Do you want to see him, Norah?"

Cass walked in front of me and stopped. Then I felt a hard tug at the back of my neck. Before I knew it, I was hoisted up into a sitting position.

It was then that I saw the full extent of what she'd had planned for me.

She stood silently near the front door, gripping the end of the rope. It was threaded through a large utility hook that she'd somehow screwed into the top of the doorframe.

Just like Donald Tisdale had.

The rope was taunt, and I knew that if Cass pulled hard enough, she could snap my neck before I ever left the ground.

"He's here, Norah. Do you want to see?"

She pointed to an area behind me, and I slowly craned my neck to follow.

I saw hands, gray, brittle hands, cupping the edge of the doorframe of Cass's bedroom.

"No," I muttered through the pain. "Please, God. No."

The hand disappeared and I saw a head, bathed in shadow, peering at me. I shut my eyes and prayed for it all to be over.

No, something else inside of me said. *I'm easy to find. And I'm always listening.*

I called out to Iris with the last bit of re-solve available to me. I feared that she wouldn't hear me, but at least I could take comfort in trying.

Please, Iris. I need you. Cassandra needs you.

I looked behind me. The head was now a full body, it's shadowy, heaving mass inching toward me.

Iris, please. Help us.

I yelped when I heard the loud knock on the door. "Norah? Cassandra?"

More frantic knocking.

Cass looked at me as if I'd somehow betrayed her. "No."

Iris was pounding on the door, but she couldn't break through. "Norah!"

I tried to call out to her but couldn't.

Then, the pounding stopped.

Oh, God. She's gone.

I closed my eyes as I felt the heaving thing closing in on me. I refused to open them, even when Cass pulled on the rope.

"You need to die so he can leave," I heard her say. "And when he leaves, they'll come back to me." Cass pulled on the rope again and I felt a burning sensation as bile shot up from the pit of my stomach and into my throat.

I could hear the rope threads stretching as she pulled again.

Then, there were stars, dancing in the darkness. And I felt more tears.

"Do it."

The heaving, monstrous thing that I refused to look at now had a voice. And it was as hideous and vile as anything I could have ever imagined.

Cass pulled again, and I felt my body rising off the floor. The rope tightened hard around my neck and was starting to cut off my air.

"Please, Cassandra. Don't do this."

I wasn't sure if I'd said the words or merely thought them. Either way, she didn't respond.

"Do it, now," that monstrous voice said. "Free me. Free yourself. Free them."

When Cass pulled the rope again, my eyes shot open, my mouth was agape in a desperate search for oxygen that wasn't there, and the muscles in my arms and legs began to seize.

In the darkness that was starting to encircle me, I heard something.

A key sliding into a lock.

Then my body hit the floor with a dull thud.

The rope was no longer tightly wound around my neck, and I could finally breathe again.

Phillip Barlow's arms were around me before I saw him. He removed the gag from my mouth, then quickly untied the knots from around my wrists and ankles.

I collapsed to the floor in anguished relief before he scooped me up and carried me to the couch.

I saw Cass standing in front of the open door, underneath that hook, staring blankly at me. The rope was still dangling from her hands.

The next sound I heard was Iris's voice.

"That's not Donald Tisdale, Cassandra. And it's not here to help you. It's something that wants to take from you. Everything that's good. And it will cajole you and trick you, until you do exactly what it wants."

"No. He's here to help me," Cass said before pulling hard on the rope. The noose end skidded harmlessly across the floor, coming to a stop near her feet.

"It's okay, Cassandra. It's over now."

Cass looked to the area where the monstrous thing had been, and her eyes grew wide with shock.

"It's gone," Iris declared.

Tears flooded Cass's eyes. "No. He was going to bring them back to me."

"They're already here," Iris said. "They've always been with you."

The room vibrated with the sound of cooing. Then...

"*It's okay, princess. Mommy's sad and we don't want her to be.*"

"But they can't stay, Cassandra," Iris said. "You have to let them go."

"I can't," Cass replied with a whimper.

"*We don't want to let you go either.*"

He appeared in the room, like a dusty image from an old film projector. His features were blurred, but I was sure he was smiling.

"This can't be," I heard from behind me.

I turned to see Phillip Barlow staring at the apparition with a mix of horror and dismay.

"There's no reason to be afraid," Iris said. The statement was directed at all of us, including Adam.

"*We can't be here, Cass. Neither can you. It's not safe.*"

I saw the life that I feared was gone instantly return to Cass's eyes.

"If I leave, will you stay with me?"

"*I'll always be with you. And so will she.*"

In the time that it took to blink. Adam was

holding Claire. She wiggled restlessly in his arms.

"*But we all have to go now.*"

"I can't let you," Cass said.

"*You have to.*"

Claire looked at the ghost of her child and began sobbing. "Will you take good care of her?"

"Forever," the apparition replied.

"And will you take good care of me?"

His features were still largely undefined, but I was positive this time that he was smiling.

"Forever and ever."

With that, Cass turned a tearful eye to Iris, then to Barlow, and finally to me.

"I'm so sorry," was all she said before collapsing where she stood.

20

A FRIENDLY FACE

It was a week later before I came back to Corona Heights. I'd left for Graham's house that night, taking only my clothes, bike, and school supplies. He had to convince me to come back for the rest.

I was initially startled when I'd seen what had become of 612. The number plate was removed and there was a plywood board blocking the door.

How was Barlow going to explain that to the residents?

Before I left for Graham's, Iris, Barlow, and I had taken Cass to the hospital. There was nothing physically wrong with her, but the staff agreed to keep her for a two-day psych hold pending her family's arrival. When I called the hospital a couple of days ago, I was informed that Cass's parents had arrived to discharge her.

I don't know what happened to her after that, but I pray on the hour, every hour, that she's safe.

Based on the number that Barlow did on this door, she definitely won't be back here. And, hopefully, neither will anyone else.

The last time I talked to him was when he agreed to let me terminate my lease early and without penalty. Even though I was appreciative of the gesture, I'd be just fine if I never saw him again.

But there was one person that I did want to see.

I made the short walk to Iris's while Graham was busy hauling boxes downstairs.

He really *was* a saint.

Iris was smiling as she opened the door. It was entirely possible that she looked through the peephole beforehand, but the expectant look on her face told me that she'd foreseen this exact moment.

"Hi, Norah,"

"Hi, Iris. How are you?"

"Better now that I've seen a friendly face. Would you like to come in?"

"I can't stay."

Iris couldn't hide her disappointment. "Right. Moving day."

"Yeah."

Her face brightened. "It's the right thing to do, and I'm glad you're doing it."

So was I.

"Looks like Barlow has boarded up 612 really good," I said.

"Something he should have done a long time ago."

"Does that mean he's finally a believer?"

"He hasn't talked to me since that night. But I get the feeling he's coming around. Time will tell."

"And what about my apartment? Do you think he'll board that up too?"

Iris thought on it for a moment, before saying, "Certainly can't hurt."

"It's still not safe in 612."

"I'm afraid not."

"Meaning that whatever was in there is still active?"

"I can't say for certain. I would've needed much more time to try to drive it away, but we had to get Cassandra out of there. Now, I won't have the chance to go back."

"I wouldn't want you in there anyway."

"It's okay, sweetheart. I've dealt with worse."

"Do you think that there are worse things here than what we saw in 612?"

"If so, they'll have to deal with me."

Iris winked and I smiled.

"What about you?" she then asked. "Where are you going from here?"

"I'm staying at my friend Graham's for a while, possibly until graduation. After that, I'll wait for the sports teams to start calling."

"They will," Iris said confidently. Then she leaned in close. "That boy is really smitten with you, isn't he?"

"How did you know that?"

"Look at you. What boy wouldn't be smitten? But watching him carrying those boxes out of the building three at a time, it was pretty obvious."

"He's a good friend, and I'd like to keep it that way. I can't afford any emotional entanglements right now."

"Don't be so sure that he's not worthy of a chance. He may be one of those snarky, intellectually-gifted hipsters, but I promise you, he's got a good heart."

My mouth flew open in amazement.

"I only listen to the really important things," Iris said in response.

"I can see that."

She extended her arms. "I feel like we've only just met, but I'm going to miss you."

I pulled her in for a tight embrace. "I'm going to miss you too."

When we were finished, I looked at her and said, "Don't be a stranger."

"You either."

"I don't think that's possible." I tapped a finger on my temple. "You're too easy to find."

The End.